D1374363

SPRINGTIME

MICHELLE
DE KRETSER

SPRINGTIME
A Ghost Story

ALLEN&UNWIN
SYDNEY · MELBOURNE · AUCKLAND · LONDON

Allen & Unwin
83 Alexander Street
Crows Nest NSW 2065
Australia
Phone: (61 2) 8425 0100
Email: info@allenandunwin.com
Web: www.allenandunwin.com

Cataloguing-in-Publication details are available
from the National Library of Australia
www.trove.nla.gov.au

ISBN 978 1 76011 121 2

Internal colour plates by Torkil Gudnason, photographer
Internal design and typesetting by Sandy Cull, gogoGingko
Printed by C&C Offset Printing Co. Ltd, China

10 9 8 7 6 5 4 3 2 1

TO SARA WHITE

THAT SPRING, Frances walked along the river every morning with her dog, Rod. One of the things that had been said in Melbourne when she announced that she was moving to Sydney was, You'll miss the parks. Other things included: There are no good bookshops there. And, What will you do for food?

Rod and Frances would cross the Wardell Road bridge and veer off onto the path that took them past the river through sports fields and parks. There were joggers and cyclists, and a girl skipping near the public barbeques. Faces grew familiar. A woman with weights attached to her wrists would say good morning, as did the Greek tailor who kept a poster of the hammer and sickle in his shop in Dulwich Hill. Frances kept an eye out for other dogs. If she saw one approaching, she swerved off the path because of Rod.

She would have said that she was heading east but sometimes found the sun skulking behind her left shoulder. Her sense of direction, moulded to Melbourne's grid, functioned by the straight line and the square. In Sydney the streets ran everywhere like something spilled. The river curved, and the sun dodged about. On a stretch of the path where there were no trees, the sun bounced off the water to punch under the brim of Frances's hat. It was a relief to arrive at the apartment block that could be seen on the escarpment, rising behind trees. Charlie's colleague Joseph lived there. He had a long terrace for the view and a tucked-away second balcony no larger than an armchair: shady all through summer, in winter it floated in light. Every day, whatever the weather, Joseph sat there for ten minutes, wind-bathing without his shirt.

His apartment block, Sixties' brown brick with a sand-coloured trim, signalled the start of Frances's favourite section of the walk. It was shaded by she-oaks, and she could look into the gardens that ran down to the path. She was still getting used to the explosive Sydney spring. It produced hip-high azaleas with blooms as big as fists. Like the shifty sun, these distortions of scale disturbed. Frances stared into a green-centred white flower, thinking, 'I'm not young any more.' How had that happened? She was twenty-eight.

For as long as she could remember, the weekend supplements of newspapers had informed her that her generation was narcissistic, spoiled, hyperconscious of brands. It was like reading about a different species. She was a solitary, studious girl, whose life had taken place in books; at least four years of it had passed in the eighteenth century. Her young parents had always treated her, their only child, as if she were more or less grown up. Her mother was French. Frances was taken to restaurants at an early age, expected to sit quietly and eat her food in a mannerly way while adults talked over her head. As a teenager, she devised a game in which she identified the sentence this or that person was least likely to utter. Her mother's was: I'm not interested in what you think, tell me what you feel.

The previous year, at a party to which Frances almost didn't go, she had met Charlie. His mother, too, was French. Charlie and Frances discovered that as children they had both called a fart a *prout*. Frances told her friends that Charlie had been unlucky in his women. After his parents divorced, his mother, a drunk, had gone home to live in a tower block in Nice.

When her son visited her, she stole from his wallet and made him massage her feet. Now, she was dead. That meant Charlie was free of her, Frances believed.

THE HOUSES BESIDE the path faced away from the river. Back gardens, lying open to the eye, hinted at private lives. At that hour of the morning, curtains were shut and decks deserted, but the aura of revelation remained. Flowers yawned, bronze-leaved cannas, lilies striped cream and red. Nasturtiums swarmed over palings. A heavy-headed datura flaunted pale orange trumpets that darkened at the rim. In September a tall, spreading tree was hung with clustered pink. A man taking a photo of it with his phone said the tree was a Queensland hardwood. Frances would have liked to photograph it too but she didn't linger here, not even when passing the ramshackle house with a flight of stone steps that reminded her of holidays in provincial France.

On this stretch of the path, hemmed in by fences and water, the difficulty was Rod. A hefty, muscled bruiser from the RSPCA, he was frightened of other dogs. Toy poodles were particularly unnerving. Coming upon a pair of them one morning, Rod tried to make a dash for the brown sludge under the mangroves. Surprised and heartened, the poodles seized the day. Telling Charlie about it, Frances said, 'Wouldn't you be frightened if tiny, angry people rushed at you shouting?' But at the time, with Rod wrenching Frances's arm and the she-oak needles slippery underfoot, no one was amused. The poodles' owner marched them on, saying, 'Come along, boys, not everyone's friendly.' Rod hung his head, screwed his paws into the ground and wouldn't budge. In the end, Frances had to pick him up and stagger past the malevolent spot recently occupied by poodle. Frances did Body Pump at the gym, but Rod weighed thirty-four kilos. In the shower, she saw red welts across her stomach where he had clawed her in fear.

The poodles had never returned. But sometimes there would be a dog in a garden – like the white bull terrier alert behind a fence. Rod's tail drooped, and his ears. Picking up her pace, Frances saw a woman in the shadowy depths of the garden. She wore a wide hat and a trailing pink dress; a white hand emerged from her sleeve. There came upon Frances a sensation that sometimes overtook her when she was looking at a painting: space was foreshortened, time stilled.

For the rest of that week, Frances kept an eye out for the bull terrier. A white stripe: danger, the surf that marks a hidden reef. But where had she seen him? Not at the French house, not at the one with the spreading tree. Had there been oleanders near the fence or a clump of banana palms? She remembered dense plantings, green gloom. The fence wasn't solid – Frances and the bull terrier had inspected each other through it – but plenty of gardens ended in railings or mesh.

Frances had pretty much forgotten the bull terrier when she saw him again. He was sniffing around a tree but lifted his head as she passed. A few days later, Rod began to whimper – the bull terrier was at his fence. Some distance behind him, the woman in the old-fashioned dress stood beside a flowering shrub. She was a sidelong glimpse through sunglasses and a coarse veil of latticework, there and gone again at once.

These partial visions, half-encounters, were repeated at intervals over weeks. One day, striding past the woman and her dog, Frances realised that whenever she saw those two she was alone on the path. The morning swayed, as duplicitous as déjà vu. When a hi-vis cyclist appeared around a bend, Frances considered hailing him – but what would she say? 'Can you see a woman in that garden?' She heard him answer, There's no one there.

FRANCES AND CHARLIE had left Melbourne so that Frances could take up a research fellowship at a university in Sydney. She was writing a book about objects in eighteenth-century French portraits. When she wasn't at the library, she worked at home, in the sunroom. Afternoons there were so dazzling that Frances had to pull down the blinds and turn on the light. The spines of her books had already dimmed. By the end of October, she needed a fan – how would she work there in summer?

The spare bedroom was reserved for Luke, who had spent three days in Sydney in September and would be returning for a week after Christmas. Charlie had left his marriage eight months after meeting Frances, and then he had left Melbourne and his young son to be with her for the rest of his life. Having more or less forgotten that she had willed these things, Frances felt their weight. Sitting at her laptop, she drew her shoulder blades together and typed, *The medieval flowers, the rose and lily of the Virgin and the Annunciation, have given way to exotics: fritillaries from Persia, dahlias from Mexico. The vase is a container that draws on great distances. The boundaries of space and time that frame human life are neutralised.* All the while, she was thinking of something that had happened when Luke came to stay. She had woken one night and found him standing by her side of the bed. When she opened her eyes, Luke asked, 'Are you dead?'

The phone rang. Frances hadn't wanted a landline. She had argued about it with Charlie, teasing and serious, saying, 'You're so twentieth century!' At last Charlie said he needed a landline so that his father could call. 'He won't ring a mobile.' His father had never called. When Frances answered the phone, there was a brief silence, and then a computer-generated female voice said, 'Goodbye.' This happened once a week or so at unpredictable times.

There had been a string of cold nights but the day was windy and hot. Walking down the passage, Frances passed through pools of cool air deliciously interspersed with warm gusts. In her study, she touched her faded books. She had amassed a good deal of information about jewels, furniture, dogs. For instance, she knew that whippets remained popular from the Middle Ages until the mid-nineteenth century. The only books Charlie read were large paperbacks with covers that showed backlit, hunted men, but when Frances told him about her research, he had seen the point of it at once: 'What people don't pay attention to changes the story.' After the party where they met, Charlie gave her a lift home, and she told him about the necessity of decentring the human subject. He had parked beside a garden where three staked camellias stood as whitely upright as martyrs. It was very cold inside the car. Soon their breath shrouded the windows, and the camellias disappeared. A phone rang. They paid no attention to it. However, several days later, days on which Charlie called her every afternoon, Frances said, 'You could come round now. But afterwards, will you feel awful?'

'You'll never know.' He said, 'I can promise you that.'

FRANCES'S PREOCCUPATIONS — Luke's next visit, her work — kept her from thinking about the woman in the old-fashioned dress. Walking beside the river pushed ideas around her mind like chairs. Sentences arrived ready-made: *Our perception, in short, is directed to the irreducible materiality of the world*. When she remembered the woman in the garden, the scene might have been a tapestry, something that existed at an angle to life. But sometimes, passing under the she-oaks, Frances found herself anticipating a figure in pink. She still couldn't pinpoint where the woman lived, so the sight of her always brought a small shock. The season was no aid to location, proliferating flowers where there had last been green drapery, or stripping away petals while buds worked loose in a neighbouring yard. For weeks, Frances placed the woman's house next door to a hand-lettered sign, fastened to a gate, that advertised ugg boots. But one morning, the sign was nowhere near when she saw a familiar shape at a fence. The woman was there too, under overhanging branches, as silent and white as her dog. Their house merged with the sun in Frances's mind: it was something else that shifted about and wasn't always where she looked.

FRANCES HAD A CHOICE of three bus routes to get to university. Charlie caught a train to the city, where he worked in IT. Sydney came to them as a series of visions held in rectangular glass. They were serious Melbourne people. They wore stylish dark coats, and Sydney could seem like an elaborate joke. T-shirts in winter! A suburb called Greystanes! On wet days, gumbooted stumps showed under the striped and sturdy domes of vast umbrellas, while subtropical rain pounded Frances and Charlie's black foldaways into collapse.

And the streetscape was so weirdly old-fashioned. Where were the hip, rusting-steel facades, Melbourne's conjuring of post-industrial decay? The decrepitude in their western suburb was real: boarded-up shops, cracked pavements, shabby terrace houses sagging behind stupendous trees. The neighbourhood had known great days before the construction of the Harbour Bridge bore the respectable away to the north shore. Traces of grandeur remained: the sandstone gate-posts that had guarded a mansion survived before a block of orange flats. Even Frances and Charlie's semi had a rising sun in the front gable to mark the dawn of the new, twentieth century, and casements edged with squares of coloured glass. This glass was engraved with flowers and tendrils. Vanished children

pressed their faces to the coloured panes to see shrubs, cars, passers-by printed with pink or blue flowers. Frances tried it for herself. She saw nothing – the glass was opaque. But later that day, she did come across some rusty steel. It was a model rocket in a playground: a relic of the Space Age, a ghost from a future that hadn't arrived.

Discovering Sydney was a way of exchanging information about each other. Charlie pointed out a bulbul in their neighbours' pomegranate tree. He googled 'Sydney birds', puzzling over a song that rose maddeningly in pitch on warm evenings. Frances called him a bird nerd. What she was really saying was, Who are you? She told him about the scrawled plea she had spotted on a wall that morning: *I am human and I need love*. They sat on the back steps drinking beer. Sunsets performed for them. Weather arrived from unexpected angles — in Melbourne, it was only necessary to look west. Charlie gathered up Frances's hair and balanced the knot on his palm. At night they slept entwined like wet sheets.

IN DECEMBER, JOSEPH invited Frances and Charlie to dinner. He led them onto the terrace, where two faces displayed sunglasses like identity-protecting black bars. They belonged to Lola and Tim – a stray plane, flying low, muffled introductions. Over the roar, Lola cried, 'Heyyy, Chaz!' They worked together, Frances learned. Why had Charlie never mentioned her? Lola lowered her voice and began to discuss something that had happened at work. Still talking to Charlie, she reached across the table and drank from Tim's glass.

An Englishwoman called Vanessa arrived, and the writer George Meshaw. When Frances was at Bryn Mawr, her father had sent her one of his novels because it had won a prize. She tried to remember whether she had finished it. George Meshaw was wearing one of those T-shirts with buttons favoured by middle-aged men – he looked as if he had been dressed by his mother.

All day a southerly had blown, but the evening was humid and still. The glass-topped table was strewn with gardenias. George fingered them, turning their petals brown. His eyes followed each dish as it was brought to the table. They were thin eyes and surprisingly inky. Eating, he grew animated, appreciative. Frances knew no writers but was acquainted with a few artists. When they weren't depressed they were drunk. George Meshaw neglected to pass the bread. He neither looked nor sounded foreign but nevertheless brought the possibility to mind.

Tim – muscles, aftershave – dealt out cards: *Tim Prescott, Creator.* He organised product launches, he explained, 'all the way from concept to creative communication outcomes'. On Frances's right, Joseph was telling Vanessa about growing up in the Soviet Union. His father, a biochemist, had spent eleven years as an exile in Kazakhstan, during which time he was known only as Object Number Six.

Before that, when Joseph was a small boy, there had been holidays in a yellow wooden dacha on a hill above the Moscow River. All day long, the children in the colony played beside the river, along the *opushka*, the edge of the forest. There was a cemetery with crosses, said Joseph, and Communist stars. When Joseph wanted to get up from the table, he placed his palms flat above his knees and pushed. Why would a man who wanted to stand exert downward pressure on his thighs?

Frances had reminded Joseph that she didn't eat meat. Joseph texted back: *No problem*. He served a platter of oysters and announced marinated duck breasts to follow. Rising to fire the barbeque, he told Frances, 'Don't worry, there is plenty of extra salad for you.' Joseph believed that if you didn't eat meat you weren't hungry. He was fifteen years older than Charlie, which made him thirty years older than Frances – older than her parents. Once he told her, 'I am one who will leave nothing behind. But you will be remembered.' Frances knew he was talking about her face and that he was wrong; she would be valued for what she had to tell the world about everything it had overlooked in eighteenth-century French paintings. Joseph invited Frances and Charlie to the opera, to the sea baths at Coogee, to picnics in blossomy parks where hidden steps led to the harbour. On a winter afternoon, he put them into his small silver car and drove them on a freeway, across the western plains, to a street where suburban villas had been transformed into Indian restaurants; the three of them sat on a terrace that had once been a garden eating spicy, delicious food. When they first met, Joseph had asked Frances if she loved the beach. When she hesitated, remembering the cold southern ocean, he said, smiling, 'You will love the beach.' His face, habitually humorous and alert, was the painter Vernet's face in the portrait by Vigée-Le Brun.

The duck breasts arrived, and a plate of coloured leaves for Frances. 'I used to be fussy about food,' remarked Vanessa. She had that penetrating, well-bred voice which, no matter what it says, enters the Australian ear like glass. 'But I was in Sri Lanka two Christmases ago. The tsunami?

When I saw what people went through, I made up my mind to always eat whatever was on my plate.'

Charlie avoided Frances's eye, just as he had avoided it when the main course was revealed. His dislike of confrontation had been a great aid to Frances in her victory, but now his incompetence as a dragon-slayer was a disappointment. Naturally, she had attributed the end of his marriage to the force of love.

Vanessa's *fortissimo* account of death, pain, horror continued. She was a GP. On hearing of the disaster, she had travelled at once to the coast. Frances tried to imagine the scenes in the makeshift hospitals – 'We ran out of analgesics pretty much straight away' – and Vanessa's clear-cut face floating above the dying like an image on a coin. When Frances thought about death, her mind blanked. The prospect of losing Charlie was the worst thing that came.

On the day Charlie left his wife, she had sent Frances an email that could still make Frances want to do unreasonable things: seize the breadknife and saw off her hair, eat stones. When Luke came to stay in September, he had brought clothes washed and folded by that witch into Frances's house. He brought spells tucked into socks. Now and then a letter arrived, redirected from Melbourne in shapely italics – the day turned black. Frances crossed her fingers to keep Charlie from uttering the three blighted syllables of her enemy's name. But Luke had her face.

Introduced to Rod, Luke had glanced at the dog and then ignored him. The next day, which Luke was to spend at the zoo after a ride on a ferry, his father couldn't get out of bed. At the airport, Charlie had hoisted his son into the air. Now his back was out. He couldn't roll over, walk or lie flat. It was a Sunday, so his osteopath couldn't be reached. He asked for Panadeine Forte. Frances didn't bother checking the bathroom cabinet. In Melbourne, Charlie had knocked on her window at five one morning. Having left his wife and son, he had left everything. He wouldn't go back, not even for his iPod or his photographs of his mother – he certainly hadn't gone back for Panadeine Forte. Lying on his side with his knees bent, Charlie didn't look ill, only old.

Luke was good about staying at home. He ate cracker biscuits spread with peanut butter and watched a *Harry Potter* DVD. His mother was known to Frances from Facebook, where she gave off a dark sparkle less like a jewel than a mine. There was no way to prove it, but Frances was sure that Luke's mother was behind the phone calls that wished her Goodbye. Her profile photos, updated regularly, showed her with a half-smile, so that her face had the empty yet powerful look of a primitive mask. The mask settled over Luke's features from time to time. The child's gestures and turns of phrase – the wrist upturned as he said, 'To be honest...' – fascinated Frances, as clues to what Charlie had once loved. Luke was a container that drew on great distances, neutralising boundaries. A cracker fell from his hand, peanut butter down, onto Frances's blue couch.

When Frances told Charlie that she was going out, his lips made a shape that might have been anything – it might have been 'Luke'. There was a small park with a playground at the end of the street. For a moment this park, which was entered through a grandiose stone arch, hung in Frances's mind. Then she clipped Rod's leash onto his collar and left the house. When she came back, an hour later, Luke was running down the passage with something in his hand. He disappeared into the room where his father lay, shouting, 'The Powerful Red Face Washer!'

'Excellent!' said a voice that vaguely resembled Charlie's. 'So now the success of our mission hangs on…the Fat Teapot of Victory.'

Luke pushed past Frances, crying, 'Sorry, chief!' as he raced for the kitchen. All the cupboards and drawers there were open. In the sunroom, the postcards that Frances kept in a biscuit tin had been disturbed. She let Rod out into the yard for a drink and returned to the bedroom. Things like a tube of sunscreen and a vase made of green glass lay on the bed. There was also a small blanket that Rod used, covered in his fur. Charlie's eyes opened when Frances spoke, but a soft, animal noise — *muh-muh-muh* — went on in his throat. In the passage Luke's footsteps grew louder, charging towards the door.

After lunch, Luke sat on the floor by the couch, murmuring over his Pokémon cards. He appeared to be counting them into piles. Frances decided to bake cupcakes. She had never made a cake. But how hard could it be? She found a recipe on the internet. It called for softened butter. There was no time to leave it sitting out of the fridge, so Frances chopped the butter into small pieces. She measured out sugar and vanilla, and started to beat them together.

Over the racket of the electric mixer, she heard Rod whine. He had left his bed in the sunroom and gone over to Luke.

The dog's ears were raised, and he was turning his head from side to side. Frances switched off the mixer. Luke was making a high, unsteady sound somewhere between a whistle and a hiss. Frances said, 'Here, Rod!' and, 'It's not a good idea to make that noise, Luke, it upsets Rod.'

'Why?'

'He thinks there's something wrong.'

'Stupid dog!'

When she switched on the mixer, Luke must have started hissing again. She saw Rod sit up on his bed and swivel his ears. He had begun to pant – a sign of stress. As soon as Frances stopped what she was doing, so did Luke. She said, keeping her voice calm, 'Please don't make that noise. I've told you why you shouldn't.'

'I didn't do anything, it was Peter Paint.' This invisible friend, who had gone away when Luke started school, had recently returned. A cup and plate had to be set for him at meals.

It went on like that for the rest of the afternoon. The child would stamp his feet or click his tongue to attract Rod, all the while watching Frances from the corner of his eye – slyly, she thought. In the end, it was easier to put Rod outside. Protesting his expulsion from the pack, Rod clawed at the flyscreen and barked.

Charlie said that Frances was over-reacting. 'Luke'll get tired of it. He's restless from being cooped up.'

'He's upsetting Rod.'

'They'll get used to each other.'

What Charlie didn't know was that the RSPCA had recommended a childless household when Frances adopted Rod. His handler said that the dog wasn't used to children – his previous owner had been an elderly man. Rod was a sweetheart but nervy. Small children made sudden gestures and noises at dog level. It was the kind of thing that appeared threatening to an animal. Frances said that she wasn't planning on having kids, so that was fine.

The conversation with Charlie was taking place in their bedroom with the door shut. Charlie lay on his side, reeking of the Tiger Balm that Frances had found in one of the Vietnamese shops on Marrickville Road. He had refused to let her touch him and had applied the ointment himself. First he held the jar at arm's length, peering at the label. He had needed reading glasses for at least six months but preferred to increase the font size on his screen. By now he was no longer making the awful noise, but his new stiff face remained. Frances hesitated between Tell me everything'll be OK and Tell me you love me – they were the same thing, she could see, which was confusing.

She had been in the room ten minutes, terrified all the time that his child would seek out Rod in the weedy yard and torture him, when Charlie said, 'Is it too early for a beer?' How did he think he was going to drink anything when he couldn't sit up? Frances knew that in Nice there had been two or three lucid hours in the morning before his mother got stuck into the gin.

When Charlie was a small boy, they would invent cocktails together when he came home from school – he was always allowed the first sip. Frances saw her face in the mirrored wardrobe: a naked, milky circle that was irresistible to chivalrous men. Outside the bedroom door, a voice said, 'Daddy, why do chairs and everything have a line around them?' Charlie spoke to his son, but his smile was for Frances. The same things amused them, and they had always been in collusion against the world.

Their house had low ceilings and dark rooms. Buses travelled past its coloured windows. The road was surfaced with concrete, which magnified the noise. Landlords who accepted pets were suspicious and rare. Frances had been required to fill out forms about Rod's age and breed, neither of which was certain. Finally, two houses came up. One was airy, pleasant and expensive. Luke's mother was a solicitor with a list of demands. Luke required Chinese herbs for his asthma, animal-print designer sneakers, fencing lessons, a soccer ball and his own computer. His father had a present waiting for him in Sydney, a Lego fire station. Luke tore at the box, but Frances saw that what he loved was a small, soft pillow he had carried onto the plane. When she sat on the floor while Luke showed her his cards, he held the pillow up between their faces if she got too close.

It made Frances feel tender towards him. But if she thought about the hours before he could be put on a plane, what stretched before her was an endless corridor with solid walls. When Charlie tapped on her window that morning in Melbourne, Frances had seen a flat, scorched landscape behind him: bodies, roofless buildings, bridges in flames. What she had left out of the picture – why? – was the prisoner taken along the way. Now the prisoner sat in front of her on dingy broadloom, and it was Frances's future that contained bars.

Her father called. She told him, speaking softly in the sunroom, about waking to find Luke by her bed. Her father said, 'How funny, it's like that dream you used to have.'

A face like a cloud came and peeped into a corner of Frances's mind. She said, 'What dream?'

'When you were four or five. You said that a man came into your room at night and bent over you when you slept. You'd always wanted your bedroom door open but then you started asking us to close it so he couldn't come in.'

Colours affected Frances. Along with the blue couch, there was a worn red leather chair in the living room. She had painted walls yellow. There were pictures. The small rooms, with their patterns and strong colours, were paintings by Matisse. Frances shifted the position of a jug that held tulips, and began to think about dinner – it was obvious that Charlie wouldn't be the one to produce it. 'Do you like pizza, Luke?' she asked.

He was watching a documentary about giraffes. 'Not frozen,' he said absently. 'Trans fats give you cancer.' His phone rang. He was six years old, and his phone cost twice as much as Frances's. Luke said, 'OK,' and 'No,' and 'It's Daddy's back again.' Moving away, Frances heard, 'Pizza,' and 'I said.' But it was the word 'again' that went through her like a wire. It alluded to a history from which she was forever banned. In addition to Luke's mother and fused vertebrae, that history held a long list of people. Some of them were called Sarah, Juliet, Anna, Daisy, Felicity and Jane. Frances had googled those with surnames. For Charlie's benefit, she produced baroque entanglements of her own and handsome, corrupt strangers. What was the use? The truth couldn't improve on a few boys as tame and necessary as hygiene, and a botched weekend with a professor who produced a school uniform he wanted her to wear in bed.

The thermostat in the oven was unreliable, and the cupcakes came out slightly burned. Inside, they were greasy in spots where the butter had melted. Luke said that Peter Paint wasn't crazy about cupcakes. Frances ate one, gave three to Rod and binned the rest. She sat on the yard steps, and Rod came and leaned against her. The dog's flat brown head, bony under her fingers, made Frances feel like crying. She saw Rod provoked, Luke bitten (a small flesh wound, a warning such as one animal delivers to another), an order for execution made out in exquisite italics. Luke's mother voted Green and didn't approve of pets. She was also careless about Facebook security. Frances knew her views on the appalling selfishness of dog-owners and the mushy way they carried on about their animals – *If the dog really could understand, it would die of shame*. That had attracted nine Likes. Frances also noticed that Luke's mother always referred to a baby as *a gorgeous bubs*. Frances didn't believe in gushing over the young of any species. She was, after all, her mother's child.

Frances put raw meat and a bone into Rod's dish. Even before she opened the back door, the dog was jumping up and down, bouncing off the cracked concrete with his legs straight. A voice from nowhere spoke: 'Please stand behind the yellow line and allow others to alight before boarding.' When Luke appeared in the doorway, Rod carried his bone to one of the weed-filled beds that edged the yard.

The Greeks next door were frying fish. Behind vertical venetians, their slinky daughter was throttling Brahms. Luke came down the steps and sat beside Frances. 'Do you like frilly music?' he asked.

In Melbourne, a magnolia had flowered outside the room where Frances lay with Charlie. Here a lemon tree grew in a circle cut out of the concrete. The lemons were small, dark yellow and hard. Rod returned to his bowl and licked it out, scraping it across the ground. He sat down and farted. Luke laughed, the sweet, bubbling laughter of young children. 'A *prout*!' said Frances. At once, the way the child was laughing changed. He sounded forced and anxious. She saw that he hadn't under-stood – why had she thought he would? The word was a gift from her mother, and his wasn't French.

On Joseph's terrace, Frances ate the last of the leaves that heaped insult on the victims of tsunamis. Vanessa was saying, 'My tattooist's just become engaged to a man she met on the internet who's got no limbs. If you're a man, some woman'll marry you even if you're basically just a head.'

George Meshaw looked at Frances. Tattooist! she heard him say. And, Where?

George leaned. His nose hung over the table. Speaking in an undertone, he said, 'You're not wearing earrings, are you?'

For a moment it was as electrifying as if he had enquired about her underwear.

In the same intimate way, he continued, 'None of the women here are wearing earrings. A couple of years ago, it would have been quite different.'

When Lola rose to help Joseph clear the table, she hooked her thumbs into her knickers and snapped their elastics. She was the kind of loud, cheerful girl men called 'gutsy' – 'busty' was what they really meant, thought Frances. There was a burn like a bar on Lola's forearm and another, now faded, on her wrist – cook's burns, inflicted by an oven. Charlie had them too, and so had his father. His father had spent the first fifteen years of his life in Hanoi. In France, he washed dishes until he ran off with his boss's girl. Before leaving Melbourne, Frances and Charlie had gone to the restaurant his father owned. After a long time, his father came downstairs. He spoke seven languages, four of them well, but chose to address his son in Mandarin, which Frances didn't understand.

With her hands full of plates, Lola said, 'So that's settled then, Chaz? You're definitely coming to my funeral?'

'For sure,' said Charlie. A beat passed. 'Obviously, if there's something really good on TV…'

Lola had polished black hair and a short geranium-red dress. Two rows of golden beads crossed on the bodice, outlining her breasts. Every shop Frances saw had racks of clothes like that – finally it had dawned on her that Sydney didn't do Summer Black. All her dark clothes had turned a dirty, green-tinged charcoal when pegged out to dry in the Sydney sun. She was wearing a Melbourne dress, a subtle sort of blue with a deep collar, and black footless tights. Her legs felt hot. The evening was a failure she traced to George Meshaw. There he sat, saying little and ruining gardenias. He seemed mesmerised by Tim, who wanted to know if George had settled on a concept for the launch of his next book. 'See, these days you have to bring your brand to life. Where I come in is I show you how to focus your message and change the paradigm.' Sincerity brought out the jut in Tim's chin. 'What you'll get is an experience that lives on after the event's over. Live webcasting, virtual styling, digital wallpaper...Have you got a blog?'

The moon rose above the trees. It had a chip on its shoulder. The scent of gardenias – not the mangled ones around George Meshaw – drifted up from the gardens across the road. There came a sound like tiny bells. Frances tapped her spoon lightly on the rim of Joseph's plate. He had phoned her one evening at the beginning of spring. 'Go outside.' The cold yard was ringing with silver music. 'What is it?' asked Frances, enchanted. Joseph didn't know. 'A beetle? A cricket? I have asked so many people, people who have lived here all their lives.'

'A monkey could do my job,' said Lola. 'But why would he want to?' George Meshaw stopped a yawn with his fist to his mouth. Vanessa had claimed Tim with the usual Sydney conversation about mortgages that disguised boasting as complaint. Her forearm, a carapace of golden bracelets, rested on the table. Then all talk ceased at the same time.

Vanessa said, 'An angel passing.'

'Or a ghost,' said Joseph. 'It's the right hour for them. When I was small, going home past the forest at the end of a summer evening, I used to see shining people between the trees. The last of the daylight on the birches, I suppose.' He looked at George. 'Do you know this idea that electricity put an end to ghost stories? People stopped seeing ghosts when rooms were properly lit.'

George Meshaw said he didn't think it was the change in lighting. 'The way stories were written changed around that time. Ghost stories work up to a shock, but the modern form of the short story is different. When a loose, open kind of story came in, writing about ghosts went out.'

A silence of a different kind fell.

Vanessa's favourite writer was Alexander McCall-Smith.

Tim's chin was of the opinion that *The Da Vinci Code* really made you think about religion.

Lola wanted to know if anyone believed in ghosts?

Frances thought, I will scream if anyone says, Isn't it funny how you never meet anyone who's actually seen a ghost?

'It's funny, isn't it,' said Vanessa, 'that ghosts always happen to other people? It's always a friend of a friend in the haunted house.' She pushed her bracelets up her arm, so that they clanged down like small, triumphant cymbals.

Frances said that she had seen a ghost. 'Near the river, in one of those gardens just down there.'

THEY WERE LYING IN BED when Charlie said, 'I still don't understand why you didn't say anything. I mean, you've been spooked for months.' His bedside lamp shone on a little stack of bright plastic; Lego bricks kept turning up in odd places, tiny red heralds of Luke's next visit or victims of the last.

'Stop it,' said Frances. 'You know I didn't really see a ghost.' What she was saying was that in wishing to provoke Vanessa, she had succeeded in frightening herself –

it was a creative communication outcome. Now she needed Charlie to explain why she was wrong. Ghosts called for calm and the application of logic. Don't tell me what you feel, tell me what you think. Vanessa had done better, declaring that of course Frances had seen a flesh-and-blood woman. Research conducted under scientific conditions had proved that ghosts were only a smell which triggered fear in the brain. Vanessa's percussive arm came down. She said, 'We haven't had a decent downpour for ages. Those mangroves were probably giving off just the right stink.'

'It's a dark, spooky sort of garden,' went on Frances. 'But Rod wasn't scared. Aren't animals supposed to be the first to sense a ghost?'

'You said Rod was terrified.'

'Of the bull terrier. You know what Rod's like. And the bull terrier wasn't frightened of the woman either.' Frances said, 'You're only upset because you think I should have told you first.'

'Is that unreasonable?'

'I don't know. Was it reasonable to ignore everyone except Lola all evening?'

'Lola! Her name's Julie.' Charlie drew his thumb across her palm, making Frances shiver. He said, 'Why do you have to do this, Fran?'

She noticed that his teeth were no longer white.

The phone rang. Charlie sprang out of bed. Frances looked at the clock: 12.37. The green numbers refused to blink. She knew she would never forget it: the precise minute when they heard that his father or hers was dead. Charlie put down the receiver without having spoken. Wearily imitative, he said, 'Goodbye.'

He left the room. The bathroom was at the other end of the house, off the kitchen. It seemed an unhygienic arrangement – surely it wouldn't have been allowed in Melbourne? Lying there with the sheet pulled over her breasts, Frances almost shouted, 'Can't you see I'm a casualty? Come back and hold me.' Twice a night, Charlie made the trek down the passage. Like failing eyesight, a weak bladder was something that showed up after you hit forty. The woman in the pink dress was over by the window, white, silent and motionless as a tomb. Frances jolted free of the muddle of sleep. She saw Joseph pushing down on his thighs in order to get up, Charlie holding a label at arm's length so that it grew clear. When she thrust Charlie away she was reclaiming him. Quite recently, on one of these occasions, he had said, 'How can I prove that I love you now? I've got nothing left to leave.'

BY THE TIME Charlie and Frances set out with Rod the next morning, the sun was golden hoops in the tops of the trees. The river had turned into fierce, colourless glass. It was a tyrant, punishing anyone who dared to look at it. Small parrots shrieked with self-importance. Their emerald broke savagely on the brassy sheen.

When they reached the she-oaks, Frances walked on ahead. She saw children on a trampoline and an Airedale bristling on a balcony. An Italianate garden came into view with terraced vegetables and lemon trees in pots. At the ugg boot sign, she began counting. Soon there was a familiar lattice fence, and unkempt shadows in the armpits of trees. Equatorial leaves sheltered the orange panting of lilies. Further back, a dark tree struck with a thousand blue eyes — a plumbago clung there and climbed towards light. But every leaf she could see was inhabited by conviction: the garden no longer resembled a dream of itself. Frances looked to the house beyond the trees for an explanation, but found only a hyperreal gable and part of a wooden rail.

Charlie came up with Rod, and they all peered through the lattice at swollen white hydrangea. At their backs, a voice swished past on racing tyres: 'Dave's really genuine.' The garden, overgrown and wild, appeared artless, but under its flickering chaos lay the bones of design. Frances pointed out a row of small trees that screened the veranda and the rear part of the garden from the path. From the house, the enclosure would resemble a stage, its backdrop greenly alive. It was there, on the threshold of the garden within the garden, that the woman in the flowing pink dress had stood, the long grass clutching at her skirt.

In plain view, the plumbago continued to climb. Frances refused to give it undue weight. 'Everything looks so normal,' she concluded.

'It looks creepy,' said Charlie. 'They've overdone the leaves.' His dead mother was speaking through him, demanding parterres, symmetry, white gravel paths.

A WEEK WENT BY. Frances and Rod toiled up the hills of Marrickville or walked the other way along the river, through Hurlstone Park.

On Sunday afternoon, Frances said that she was going to the gym. In the street where Joseph lived, she parked in front of the house that sold ugg boots. She set off along the street, counting. It was strange to discover the faces of houses grown familiar from behind, like seeing friends assume stiff, public facades.

She came to a small garden planted with grevilleas and delicate flowering gums. Light dropped through their leaves, creating an airy brightness quite un-like the dense shade at the back. Birds sang. One asked a question. A long ripple passed through Frances, head to heel. She looked back at the deserted Sunday street — she could reach her car in a minute — and opened the gate.

Soft, bad music was leaking onto the porch through the screen door. Frances pushed up her sunnies and rang the bell. Soon a form took shape in the dimness, pixelated with fine wire mesh. The woman was gathering up her hair — it was glori-ous hair, a bright brown mass. On the other side of the door, with her arms still raised,

'Can I help you?' she said, like someone in a shop.

Frances had on the blue dress she had worn to Joseph's dinner. Loosely cut, it fell straight down and gave her the look of a waif. She said, 'Excuse me for interrupting your afternoon. I live just near here' — waving a vague, westerly hand. 'My partner and I moved up to Sydney recently and we're establishing our garden. We're not too familiar with the plants up here, and I saw those gorgeous orange flowers you've got at the back. Could you please tell me what they're called?'

The woman said, 'Hang on,' and opened the door. Lightly tanned, she had round lids sculpted over shallow-set eyes. If she had been beautiful, she would have resembled this or that famous painting, but her heavy face was ordinary. 'My husband's the one you want – he's the gardener. But he's taken the girls to the beach.'

'Would your mother know?' asked Frances.

'My *mother*?'

The cold hand played its scale down Frances's spine. She heard a voice say, My mum's been gone ten years. Before it could, she rushed on. 'A friend maybe? I've seen her out the back. In a long pink dress.'

When the woman laughed, her brown cheeks shook. Frances put her hand to her face. The plumbago rose behind her eyes, unearthly blue in borrowed leaves. She looked down. She saw broad, bare feet, and toenails painted a vehement red.

The flesh bulged around a sliver of nail on one big toe.

'Sorry, sorry. I'm being rude.' The woman pushed the screen door wide. 'Come in. I'll show you. It's easier. You'll see.'

The passage was gloomy after the over-bright afternoon – Frances almost collided with a hallstand. But as soon as she stepped inside, she knew that Charlie was wrong. Like the woman ushering her along with 'So where did you move here from?' and 'Oh, I love Melbourne!' and 'How are you finding it here?', the house was friendly and banal.

The living room, congested with Smooth FM, confirmed her assessment. Frances took in a plastic Christmas tree flashy with tinsel, and the gleaming black expanse of a wall-mounted TV. A French window showed a paved path running down one side of the house. She wondered if the silent bull terrier would appear – Rod would have barked like crazy at the sound of the gate. But presumably the dog, too, had gone to the beach.

The woman crossed to an archway, saying, 'Through here,' and, 'Don't look at the mess. I thought I'd make a start on wrapping the kids' presents while they're out of the way.'

The far end of the second room was a kitchen. In front of Frances were shopping bags, scissors, parcels, a teapot, a sticky-tape dispenser and long rolls of coloured paper – all this entered her eye as a brilliant blur.

She was looking past the dining table, past the bifolds that gave onto the garden. A familiar figure was waiting in a corner. Here and there, her white skin was chipped.

'Meet Sybil,' said the woman. 'The girls have always got some game going on with her. But then they go and leave her outside overnight. They'll be rapt you thought she was real.' She stepped around the mannequin and peered at the garden. 'So where did you say these flowers were exactly?'

When Frances had written down her mobile number with one digit altered, she walked back up the passage to the front door. There was a row of photos on the stand in the hall: a square, red man, two plain children with abundant hair. Also the

73

bull terrier. A label, printed in crayon, was stuck to the bottom of his frame: *Hector.*

On the porch, relieved, foolish, guilty, Frances overdid her thanks.

'No worries, it was a pleasure,' said the woman. 'I'll get Craig to text you as soon as he's back.' She leaned out to pluck a brown leaf from a begonia in a pot.

Frances said, 'I'll give Sybil and Hector a wave the next time I see them.' She saw the big, smiling face freeze.

ON A FEBRUARY EVENING eight years later, Frances sat in a gate lounge at Sydney airport. Storms had delayed her flight home to Melbourne. Her laptop was open – she should have been working on an application to fund her new book on eighteenth-century gardens, but her mind kept flicking about. The cancer had probably started in Joseph's liver; three weeks from diagnosis to death. Frances had been in Paris doing research. The previous day, she had returned from exhausted

winter to shocking blue skies. Delirious
with jetlag and light, she listened to her
messages: there was one from Joseph asking her to call him, and one from a stranger
named Irina telling her he had died.

After a white night, Frances had risen
early to catch a plane to Sydney. The
funeral was slow in getting started. People
stood about under gaudily striped umbrellas outside the church in Centennial
Park – the priest was late or the key was
lost. A pattern of grapes and vine leaves ran
across the top of the iron gates. The air was
as heavy and damp as Frances's shoes. Thick
rain blew in under the cheap black brolly
she had bought at Central. On the way to
the airport that morning, on the plane, she
had held pictures of Sydney in February

in her mind: the sinister spider lilies that appeared overnight, the crepe myrtles like extravagant bouquets. Why had she forgotten how it rained?

St Vladimir's was really a single-storey house. It brought to mind a different house, far away in the west, a sparkling Sunday in winter and a waiter carrying out a tray of small brass bowls. They had stayed on that terrace all afternoon, Joseph, Frances and Charlie, drinking Kingfishers and talking about travelling to Russia together. When it grew dark, a red neon star over the restaurant sprang into life. She had learned a new word: *podvypevshii*. It meant something like 'gently drunk'.

The wind came and ran its hands over the trees, and Frances turned her back on the rain. The other mourners, about twenty people dressed like her in dark clothes, seemed to be Russians of Joseph's generation. To whom was she to offer condolences? Irina had identified herself as a friend of Joseph's. 'Friend' could mean anything, an accomplice, a rival. Irina's accent was so clotted that at first Frances had thought she was saying she was afraid of Joseph. She remembered a story he had told: when the man, a fellow scientist, who had denounced his father died, Joseph's mother wrote to his widow, signing off *with deepest respect*. 'It is what we say in Russia when all respect is gone.'

A long car came into view, moving at a stately pace. The people waiting stirred like leaves. When they began their wavering procession into the church, Frances followed slowly. The internet had informed her that at Russian funerals the coffin was left open. She watched Joseph stroll ahead, down sandstone steps to the waiting water. Then she followed him past iron grapes.

In the entranceway, a short woman came forward: 'You are Frances?' She offered a velvety, veined hand. 'Irina.' Frances saw a boldly red fringe under a sombre scarf, the pouchy Russian doll's face. The two women moved into the church. The walls were crowded with icons, and there were no chairs. Spacy with sleeplessness, Frances remarked on the contrast. Irina said, 'Who would sit in the presence of God?' Her grey eyes were the colour of smoked glass.

Around six, the rain had thinned and finally stopped. Two hours later, airline schedules were still in turmoil with dozens of flights backed up. The gate-lounge window was showing a spectacular amber and mauve sky. On a long-ago evening, the same colours, full of tenderness and promise, had presided over Charlie and Frances when Joseph took them to an open-air cinema by the harbour. As the sky darkened, lights came on: some steadfast, some winking, on the far shore, on the water. Frances tightened her hold on Charlie's hand. Why were lights seen in the darkness so moving? All at once, massive wheels were thundering towards her out of a snowy night – the train seemed to have risen from the harbour. A week later, Frances had forgotten pretty much everything about the film, but what did that matter? It was cinema as wonder, as she hadn't experienced it since childhood. In the gate lounge, Joseph's kindness was vividly present, the outings that were astonishments, the lovely city giving up its secrets, one by one like a box of delights.

Frances saved her grant application and closed the file. Her screensaver came up: a photo of Rod, sitting on his tailbone, grinning in a concrete yard. Behind him, a row of staked greenery was visible. Frances and Charlie had cleared the north-facing bed and planted tomatoes. Melbourne-bred, they failed to consider fruit flies. Their tomatoes looked luscious and tasted foul. These days, Rod filled a square silver tin on Frances's mantelpiece. She had thought that the time when the photo had power over her had passed but discovered that she was wrong.

She packed away her laptop and went in search of a drinking fountain. At once her seat was claimed by a girl with peppermint-green hair. People were sitting on the floor, in the walkways. In France, a revolution would have been brewing: a leader risen from the people, briefcases wielded like cobblestones, authority hunted out and harangued with the trenchant platitudes of TV intellectuals. Australians chatted to their phones, ate food from vending machines, read magazines with exclamation marks in their titles. Resentment was reserved for the powerless: directed in glares at the mother whose baby wouldn't hush, at the cleaner wheeling a bin from whose path luggage had to be cleared.

A disembodied voice announced that a flight was ready for boarding. A queue, which had already formed in anticipation, lengthened and advanced. Then it halted. The voice said, 'Would Daniela Gregson, travelling to Perth on Qantas flight 568, please make yourself known to staff in the gate lounge? Paging passenger Daniela Gregson.'

The queue stirred in its depths and disgorged a tall woman in a pastel dress – the glares followed her, too. Frances scanned her: a glamorous stranger with a broad red bangle and gym-toned arms. Then she realised, Not a stranger. Daniela Gregson had lost weight, and her hair, streaked with gold, was now a dense, wavy bob. She looked, improbably, younger than when Frances had met her – in fact, was it the same woman? Frances's eyes passed down a pale-blue body to a brown foot advancing in a wedge-heeled sandal: the sliver of toenail was painted pink. So much had changed since Frances had first seen that foot that a paradigm couldn't cover it, but what Daniela Gregson told her had never gone away. The downward turn of Frances's life had already begun but this wasn't apparent to her yet. Long after it was, many years later, the senseless phrase 'Hector died last summer' would persist. Frances caught sight of her face, smoothed and briefly creepy, in the dark background of a lightwall advertising a bestseller. She went into the airport bookshop and took out her phone. She texted George Meshaw: *Just learned the name of Hector's owner.* She was really saying, Tell me everything'll be OK. She was saying, Tell me there are no ghosts.